William Cullen Bryant

The Story of the Fountain

Anatiposi

William Cullen Bryant

The Story of the Fountain

Reprint of the original, first published in 1872.

1st Edition 2023 | ISBN: 978-3-38218-320-2

Anatiposi Verlag is an imprint of Outlook Verlagsgesellschaft mbH.

Verlag (Publisher): Outlook Verlag GmbH, Zeilweg 44, 60439 Frankfurt, Deutschland
Vertretungsberechtigt (Authorized to represent): E. Roepke, Zeilweg 44, 60439 Frankfurt, Deutschland
Druck (Print): Books on Demand GmbH, In de Tarpen 42, 22848 Norderstedt, Deutschland

The Story of the Mountain

THE
STORY OF THE FOUNTAIN.

BY

WILLIAM CULLEN BRYANT.

Illustrated with Forty-two Engravings on Wood.

NEW YORK:

D. APPLETON & COMPANY

MDCCCLXXII.

Entered, according to Act of Congress, in the year 1871 by

D. APPLETON & CO.,

In the Office of the Librarian of Congress, at Washington.

THE STORY OF THE FOUNTAIN.

FOUNTAIN, that springest on this grassy slope,
Thy quick cool murmur mingles pleasantly,
With the cool sound of breezes in the beech,
Above me in the noontide.

Thou dost wear

No stain of thy dark birthplace; gushing up
From the red mould and slimy roots of earth,
Thou flashest in the sun.   The mountain-air,
In winter, is not clearer, nor the dew
That shines on mountain-blossom.   Thus doth God
Bring, from the dark and foul, the pure and bright.

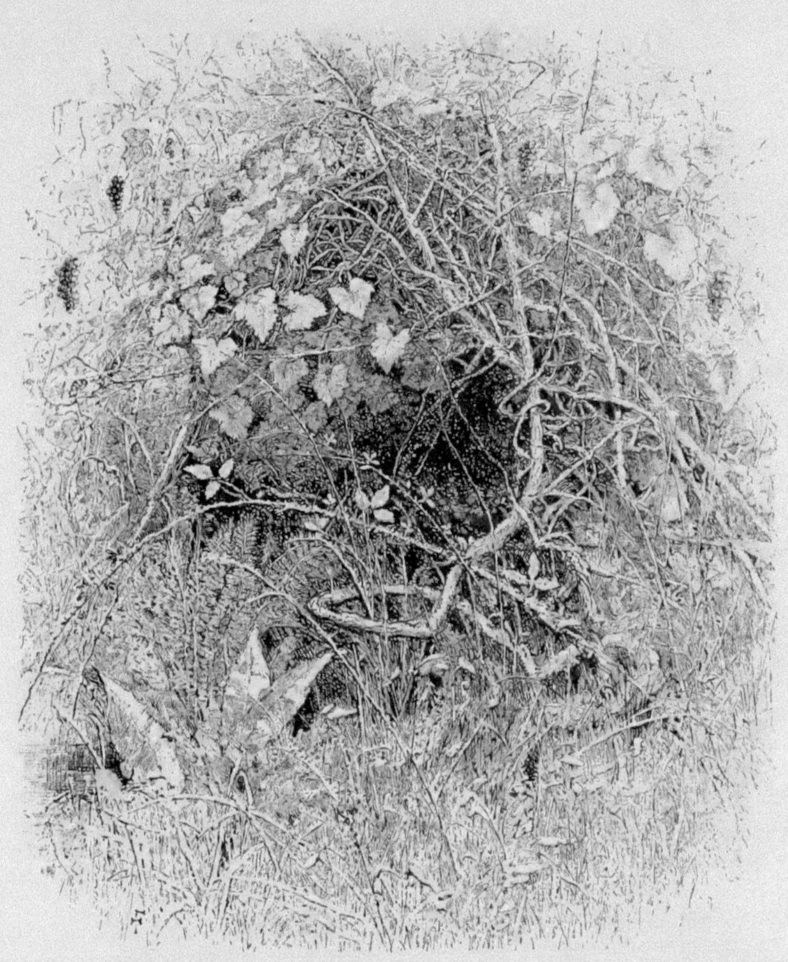

This tangled thicket on the bank above
Thy basin, how thy waters keep it green!
For thou dost feed the roots of the wild vine
That trails all over it, and to the twigs
Ties fast her clusters.

There the spice-bush lifts
Her leafy lances; the viburnum there,
Paler of foliage, to the sun holds up
Her circlet of green berries.

In and out
The chipping sparrow, in her coat of brown,
Steals silently, lest I should mark her nest.

Not such thou wert of yore, ere yet the axe
Had smitten the old woods.   Then hoary trunks
Of oak, and plane, and hickory, o'er thee held
A mighty canopy.   When April winds

Grew soft, the maple burst into a flush
Of scarlet flowers.

The tulip-tree, high up,
Opened, in airs of June, her multitude
Of golden chalices to humming-birds
And silken-winged insects of the sky.

Frail wood-plants clustered round thy edge in Spring.
The liver-leaf put forth her sister blooms
Of faintest blue.

Here the quick-footed wolf,
Pausing to lap thy waters,
   crushed the flower
Of sanguinaria, from whose
   brittle stem
The red drops fell like blood.

The deer, too, left

Her delicate footprint in the soft moist mould,
And on the fallen leaves.

The slow-paced bear,
In such a sultry summer noon as this,
Stopped at thy stream, and drank, and leaped across.

But thou hast histories that stir the heart
With deeper feeling; while I look
on thee
They rise before me.
I behold the scene
Hoary again with
forests;
I behold

The Indian warrior, whom a hand unseen
Has smitten with his death-wound in the woods,
Creep slowly to thy well-known rivulet,
And slake his death-thirst.   Hark, that quick fierce cry

That rends the utter silence; 'tis the whoop
Of battle, and a throng of savage men
With naked arms and faces stained like blood,
Fill the green wilderness.   The long bare arms

Are heaved aloft, bows twang and arrows stream;
Each makes a tree his shield, and every tree
Sends forth its arrow.   Fierce the fight and short,
As is the whirlwind.   Soon the conquerors

And conquered vanish, and the dead remain
Mangled by tomahawks.   The mighty woods
Are still again, the frighted bird comes back
And plumes her wings; but thy sweet waters run
Crimson with blood.

> Then, as the sun goes down,
> Amid the deepening twilight I descry
> Figures of men that crouch and creep unheard,
> And bear away the dead.   The next day's shower
> Shall wash the tokens of the fight away.

I look again—a hunter's
    lodge is built,
With poles and boughs, beside thy
    crystal well,
While the meek Autumn stains the woods
    with gold,
And sheds his golden sunshine.

To the door

The red-man slowly drags the enormous bear
Slain in the chestnut-thicket, or flings down
The deer from his strong shoulders.   Shaggy fells
Of wolf and cougar hang upon the walls,

And loud the black-eyed Indian maidens laugh,
That gather, from the rustling heaps of leaves,
The hickory's white nuts, and the dark fruit
That falls from the gray butternut's long boughs.

So centuries passed by, and still the woods
Blossomed in spring, and reddened when the year
Grew chill, and glistened in the frozen rains
Of winter, till the white man swung the axe

Beside thee—signal of a mighty change.
Then all around was heard the crash of trees,
Trembling awhile and rushing to the ground,

The low of ox, and shouts of men who fired
The brushwood, or who tore the earth with ploughs.

The grain sprang thick and tall, and hid in green
The blackened hill-side ;

Ranks of spiky maize
Rose like a host embattled;

The buckwheat
Whitened broad acres,

Sweetening with its flowers
The August wind.   White cottages were seen
With rose-trees at the windows ; barns from which

Came loud and shrill the crowing of the cock ;

Pastures where rolled and neighed the lordly horse,
And white flocks browsed and bleated.   A rich turf

Of grasses brought from far o'ercrept thy bank,
Spotted with the white clover.

Blue-eyed girls
Brought pails, and dipped them in thy crystal pool;

38

And children, ruddy-cheeked and flaxen-haired,
Gathered the glistening cowslip from thy edge.

Since then, what steps have trod thy border!   Here
On thy green bank, the woodman of the swamp
Has laid his axe, the reaper of the hill
His sickle, as they stooped to taste thy stream.

The sportsman, tired with wandering in the still
September noon, has bathed his heated brow
In thy cool current.

Shouting boys, let loose
For a wild holiday, have quaintly shaped
Into a cup the folded linden-leaf,
And dipped thy sliding crystal.

From the wars

Returning, the plumed soldier by thy side
Has sat, and mused how pleasant 'twere to dwell
In such a spot, and be as free as thou,
And move for no man's bidding more.   At eve,

When thou wert crimson with the crimson sky,
Lovers have gazed upon thee, and have thought
Their mingled lives should flow as peacefully

And brightly as thy waters.   Here the sage,
Gazing into thy self-replenished depth,
Has seen eternal order circumscribe
And bind the motions of eternal change,
And from the gushing of thy simple fount
Has reasoned to the mighty universe.

Is there no other change
          for thee, that lurks
Among the future ages?
          Will not man
Seek out strange arts to wither
          and deform
The pleasant landscape which
          thou makest green?
Or shall the veins that feed
          thy constant stream
Be choked in middle earth,
          and flow no more
For ever, that the water-plants
          along
Thy channel perish, and the
          bird in vain
Alight to
          drink?

Haply shall these green hills

Sink, with the lapse of years, into the gulf

Of ocean-waters, and thy source be lost

Amidst the bitter brine ?   Or shall they rise,

Upheaved in broken cliffs and airy peaks,
Haunts of the eagle and the snake, and thou
Gush midway from the bare and barren steep?

48